To Nathan, Nicole, and Gwen
—J.J.

For Maguire and Carter
—B.S.

Text copyright © 2016 by Jory John
Jacket art and interior illustrations copyright © 2016 by Bob Shea

All rights reserved. Published in the United States by Random House Children's Books,
a division of Penguin Random House LLC, New York.
Random House and the colophon are registered trademarks of Penguin Random House LLC.

Visit us on the Web! randomhousekids.com
Educators and librarians, for a variety of teaching tools, visit us at RHTeachersLibrarians.com

Library of Congress Cataloging-in-Publication Data is available upon request.

ISBN 978-0-385-38990-7 (trade) — ISBN 978-0-385-38991-4 (lib. bdg.) — ISBN 978-0-385-38992-1 (ebook)

MANUFACTURED IN CHINA
10 9 8 7 6 5 4 3 2 1
First Edition

Book design by John Sazaklis

Random House Children's Books supports the First Amendment and celebrates the right to read.

QUIT CALLING ME A MONSTER!

JORY JOHN
wrote the words

BOB SHEA
drew the pictures

RANDOM HOUSE 🏠 NEW YORK

**Quit calling me a monster!
Just . . . stop it, right this minute!**

Just because I have a huge,
toothy smile that
glows in the dark.

Just because
I roar.

And whoop.

And
scream.

And cackle.

And
holler.

And howl at the moon.

And howl at the sun.

Just because I hide under the bed . . .

. . . or at the back of the closet . . .

. . . or behind the shower curtain . . .

. . . or in the glove compartment.

It really bothers me when you call me
a monster without even thinking about it.

"There goes a monster!"
you exclaim when
I pass by.

"Mommy, save me from that monster!"
you holler when I'm just trying
to get some groceries.

"I think there's a monster under my bed!"
you scream when I'm just trying to sleep.

Okay, so maybe I let my claw slip out.
And maybe I growl in my sleep.
But it's not my fault.

You should see *you* when you sleep.

It's all so very annoying.
It's not like I ever call you names, do I?

I could easily be like,
"Look at that little meat
snack over there."

Or "There goes the kid I'm going to chomp up."

But I don't.
I don't say anything. Because I have good manners.
You could really learn something from me.

Yep. I'm a monster with excellent manners!

Um . . . I didn't mean . . .
I didn't mean *monster,* exactly . . .
I'm not a . . . um . . .

Sigh.

Okay, okay. Okay! I'm *technically* a monster.

After all, I have horns. And fangs. And wild eyes.
And crazy hair. And clompy feet. And long toenails.
And a huge, toothy smile that glows in the dark.

And my *parents* are monsters.
It's all kind of obvious, I guess.

Still, I really don't like being called
a monster one bit.

How would you like it?

You wouldn't—*that's* how.

So quit calling me a monster,
everyone.

My name is Floyd.
Floyd Peterson.

Please call me Floyd Peterson from now on and I won't roar at you like this.
ROARRRRRRRRRRRRRR!

Or this . . .
GROWLLLLLLLLLLLLL!
Or this . . .
KAIYAWWWWWWWWWW!

That's the roar of Floyd Peterson.
Not bad, right?

Now I'm going to bed.

Try not to wake me when you clomp in
with your silly feet. No offense.

ROAR

SNORE

ROAR

SNORE

Much better.